LYTTLE LiES

THE PUDDING PROBLEM

JOE BERGER

LIBRARIES
WITHDRAWN FROM STOCK

SIMON & SCHUSTER

LONDON   NEW YORK   TORONTO   SYDNEY   NEW DELHI

The Den.

Designed to blend in with the natural surroundings of my bedroom. It may not look like much from the outside, but appearances can be deceptive. Inside it's custom-engineered for maximum quietness, relaxation and alone-time.

Only authorized personnel are allowed within its hallowed walls – those issued with a personal ID card.

NAME:
Charlie Beans

STATUS:
Best friend

SKILLS:
Coolness in the face of a) peril, b) my big sister. Ability to see things that others can't.

DISTINGUISHING FEATURES:
Hair. Lots of hair. Eyes? No one's sure.

NAME:
Pudding

STATUS:
Cat

DISTINGUISHING FEATURES:
Purring. Big Eyes.

KNOWN ISSUES:
Speed eating. Iffy bladder control. Tendency to panic.

The Den is the perfect place to escape the many stresses and strains imposed on the modern nine-year-old. I'm not talking about the more extreme problems that occasionally crop up. Like the time aliens attacked our town and abducted practically everyone …

…until I discovered the invaders were allergic to cucumbers and single-handedly saved the day with a cardboard tube and a jar of out-of-date gherkins.

Or the time a sinkhole opened up in the middle of assembly, right under the Year Twos ...

... and I had to be lowered down on a rope to rescue them all because the head teacher was crying in the corner. (He's not a fan of sinkholes.)

HEAD TEACHER. →
SERIOUSLY WEIRD.

No, the kinds of stresses I'm talking about are your typical, everyday, run-of-the-mill-type concerns:

Big sisters who are **sooo** superior and annoyingly good at everything that it makes you look kind of rubbish in comparison.

Mums who think maths homework is the sole purpose of being a child...

Dads who think constant jazz-guitar noodling is the perfect accompaniment to maths homework...

... And, of course, the many false accusations of terrible crimes. I'm sure you get the same stuff...

The house nearly burned down – AGAIN! It must be SAM!

There are carrots actually *growing* in the apple tree! SAM!

A melted tennis ball full of cheese has been found in the microwave – the Kitchen Police are appealing for witnesses and would like to speak to (guess who?) SAM!

PING!

Okay, it's possible you don't get this as much as me.
You see, I have this **'REPUTATION'** thing.

And a reputation is always a bad thing.

It's like having a sign around your neck that says:

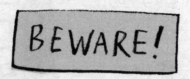

You can have a reputation for all sorts of things, but mine is for one thing in particular: I have been known to tell the odd porky-pie.

It has been suggested that the truth rarely troubles my lips.

On occasion, I may have said something that turned out to have a less than firm basis in fact.

To put it another way, the sign around my neck says ...   And the one on my forehead ...

In fact, if you look very closely, you'll start to see little signs all around me. . .

You see, the TRUTH of the matter is … well, the truth is complicated. Complicated like … an elephant.

Imagine you're pootling along on your motorized skateboard,

or Segway,

or hoverboard.

SOMEONE NEEDS TO INVENT THIS NOW. QUICKLY!

There you are, pootling along happily, when all of a sudden there's this huge ELEPHANT in the middle of the road.

It's looking at you in a funny way. You start to feel nervous – it's just too big to deal with.

You can't go under it, or over it (even on a hoverboard), but you can skirt round it. Simple!

You get to go about your business and the elephant (or, the truth) gets to stay there being all complicated. Everybody's happy!

In any case, it's not like I'm the only person around here whose record with the facts is not one-hundred-percent spotless.

← GRANDPA,
AKA THE GREAT
WONDEROSO

Grandpa lives with us, although most of the time he's down on his allotment, growing stuff – like radishes.

He does the most amazing magic tricks. And magic is basically lying, isn't it? It's saying things happened when they didn't, and saying things didn't happen when they did.

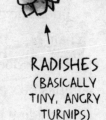

RADISHES
(BASICALLY
TINY, ANGRY
TURNIPS)

So, when Grandpa turns
a box of matches into a
glass of orange juice,

or a whole deck
of cards into rose
petals,

or takes the watch off
Dad's wrist while he's
playing the guitar ...

... does he get told off and sent to sit on the 'thinking chair'?

No, he doesn't – he gets oohs and aahs and everyone thinks he's amazing.

Including me.

And, at the other end of the lying-spectrum, there's...
Ugh, gives me the shivers even saying his name.

FEENY

FEENY'S
HELL HOUND,
BUTCHER.

Pete 'three strikes' Feeny. He's the class bully and
actually one of the worst people in the world.

(Don't tell him I said that.)

And he's the biggest liar there is. In front of Miss Magpie, he's always helpful and polite and volunteers for everything in class.

And, as soon as her back is turned, the REAL Feeny comes out.

When he's got it in for you, his eyes go dead, like a shark's.

I can't actually bring myself to look at them.

ARTIST'S IMPRESSION
OF THE 'DEAD EYE'.
(DO NOT LOOK AT THIS
PICTURE FOR TOO LONG.)

They call him '**Three Strikes Feeny**' because, if you cross him three times, it's curtains for you.

You want to know what 'curtains' looks like?

CARL
CURTAINS $\longrightarrow$

He was once the most popular boy in school, until the time he crossed Feeny's path – three times in the same day! Carl no longer attends Parsley Primary, but, wherever he is, he'll never be the same again.

So, as you can see, with all the everyday stresses of life, I'm in desperate need of The Den. And right now I need it more than ever. I'm in a pickle. In fact, I'm in a whole JAR of pickles. It's four o'clock on Friday, and I've got until Monday morning to sort it out, or ELSE!

Actually, I suppose the proper
beginning was months ago and, perhaps
unsurprisingly, it started with a lie. But it
was a good lie – one that helped everyone
out. Well, nearly everyone.

The
IMAGINARY
CHEESEBURGER
LIE*

*Is a lie still a lie if you tell it to *yourself*?

Every day, in the school canteen, I watch with a mixture of envy, longing and downright misery as Pete Feeny opens his lunch box.

See, Pete's stepsister works in a burger bar. And every day at noon she drops off Pete's lunch at school in a brown paper bag. And, every lunchtime, it's the same thing...

A BIG
FAT
HOT
JUICY
CHEESEBURGER.

SLOW MOTION

When I can't stand it any more, I look away and turn my attention to my own packed lunch. I always say a little prayer before I open it.

And every day, my prayers go unanswered.

My lunch always contains the same core ingredients.

Exhibit A: Bottle of (drumroll, please) WATER! A single-source, unblended water (from our kitchen tap).

Exhibit B: OLD apple. How do I know it's old? Because every day I carve a little notch on it.

Okay, those I could live with if it weren't for the main event, the *pièce de résistance*…

Exhibit C: Two dry slices of thick, super-wholemeal bread, with a seam of sweaty cheddar cheese running through the middle.

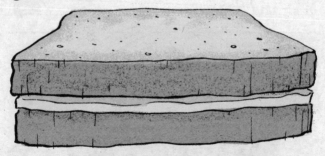

EVERY day. Same thing.

Charlie tries to sympathize…

YEAH, I KNOW WHAT YOU MEAN …
I GET THE SAME STUFF EVERY DAY TOO: A POT
OF POTATO SALAD, LITTLE POT OF HOUMOUS,
CHOPPED CARROT AND CUCUMBER FOR DIPPING,
PITTA BREAD STUFFED WITH FALAFEL, ROAST
CHICKEN LEG, PACKET OF CRISPS, FLASK OF TEA,
CHOCOLATE BISCUITS WITH MINT CRÉME, POT OF
TOFFEE-FLAVOURED YOGHURT, CHOPPED BANANA
WITH HONEY AND CHOCOLATE SPRINKLES …

CHARLIE…

YUP?

SWAP A CHICKEN LEG
FOR THIS APPLE?
IT'S A SIX-NOTCHER.

YOU KNOW WHAT?
I'LL DO IT … IF ONLY TO
PUT THAT POOR APPLE
OUT OF ITS MISERY.

SWIPE!

TOSS!

Thing is, I don't blame my mum. She has enough to cope with, what with her jazz allergy, and my sister being such a high-maintenance high achiever and everything.

But I do eventually have to mention it to Grandpa.

THE NEXT MORNING

So I keep my promise. All morning I want to peek, but I don't. By lunchtime, my mind is whirring, my tummy's rumbling... And I carefully lift the lid.

It's all been a **SICK JOKE**.

My lunchbox contains the usual suspects:

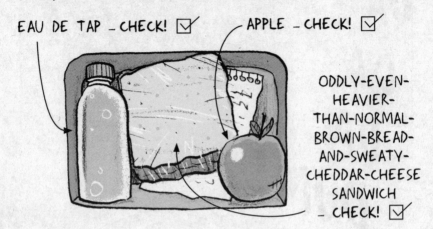

EAU DE TAP – CHECK! ☑

APPLE – CHECK! ☑

ODDLY-EVEN-
HEAVIER-
THAN-NORMAL-
BROWN-BREAD-
AND-SWEATY-
CHEDDAR-CHEESE
SANDWICH
– CHECK! ☑

However, underneath it all, a note:

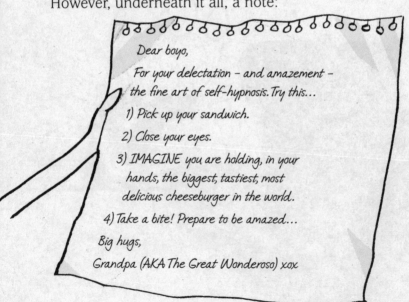

Dear boyo,

For your delectation – and amazement –
the fine art of self-hypnosis. Try this...

1) Pick up your sandwich.

2) Close your eyes.

3) IMAGINE you are holding, in your
hands, the biggest, tastiest, most
delicious cheeseburger in the world.

4) Take a bite! Prepare to be amazed...

Big hugs,

Grandpa (AKA The Great Wonderoso) xox

So the next lunchtime, with nothing to lose but my sweaty cheddar, I decide to give it a go.

BUDGE UP, WILL YOU?

GRRR...

WHAT ARE YOU DOING?

IT'S AN EXPERIMENT. COULD I PLEASE GET A BIT OF PEACE AND QUIET?

OH, OKAY, SURE...

So, with all eyes firmly on me...

LIMBERING UP ...

FINGER STRETCHES ...

DEEP BREATH ...

FOCUS ...

MUNCH

MUNCH

41

43

Everyone starts doing it...

And I'm the hero of lunchtime, all thanks to Grandpa and the power of the mind.

Until...

Pete Feeny decides he wants in on the action.

But in all the excitement, he must have forgotten what was already in his lunch bag. You'll remember I told you about his sister's burger bar and Feeny's lunch:

big

    fat

        hot

           juicy

               cheeseburger...

Now, I don't want to get too technical here ... but when Feeny closes his eyes and imagines eating a big, fat, hot, juicy cheeseburger, and then takes a bite out of what is *in fact* a big, fat, hot, juicy cheeseburger, it causes something called a:

CLOSED-LOOP
FEEDBACK CONTINUUM

(Grandpa tells me afterwards this is something to watch out for – great, thanks for the heads-up, Grandpa.)

Which causes a chain reaction ...

... which causes Feeny's head to explode.

Okay, so it turns out, after the air clears, that Feeny's head hasn't actually exploded – he's just been really badly sick everywhere. Which causes several other kids to lose their imaginary cheeseburgers too. Which weirdly look a lot like how you'd imagine a real cheeseburger might...

Well, anyhow, it isn't terribly nice. And Feeny isn't terribly happy.

Then there's a noise.

SKWEE SKWEE *SKWEE...*

Every child in the school knows this noise.

SKWEE SKWEE SKWEE...

It's the
**head
teacher.**

The head is super
weird – he's obsessed
with flowers. He
goes everywhere
with a sharp pair
of secateurs and
the angrier he
gets, the more
he squeezes them. Even
Feeny is freaked out by
him.

SKWEE
SKWEE
SKWEE

Kids who get into big trouble are forced to join the
head's 'Garden Gang' – they spend all break and
lunchtimes helping weed and prune, and shovelling
manure in the rose garden.

SKWEE
SKWEE
SKWEE

It's every child's worst nightmare.

To make it truly horrible, they have to eat lunch with him too – edible flowers and leaves they've harvested.

Needless to say, the head is not happy with all the sick, and issues a **TOTAL BAN** on cheeseburgers, real or imaginary. This particularly affects Feeny, and he seems to think it's all my fault. His eyes do that thing, and I have to look away.

Oops! Where was I?

Oh, that's right – in trouble **AGAIN**.

Wolfe Stone is my favourite TV show, and Charlie's too.

WOLFE STONE

STONE IS A MAVERICK CRIME-FIGHTER WHO IS ALWAYS GETTING IN TROUBLE WITH HIS SUPERIORS.

HE IS LITERALLY OBSESSED WITH TRUTH AND JUSTICE – JUST LIKE ME.

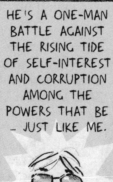

HE'S A ONE-MAN BATTLE AGAINST THE RISING TIDE OF SELF-INTEREST AND CORRUPTION AMONG THE POWERS THAT BE – JUST LIKE ME.

HE HAS A COOL MOTORBIKE, MIRRORED SHADES AND STUBBLE.

(THESE ARE ALL ON NEXT YEAR'S CHRISTMAS LIST.)

That's my sis – always looking out for me.

I don't like where this is heading...

She's good, my sister. She's no slouch. But neither am I.

HEY, BOB! LONG TIME NO SEE! HOW ARE THE WIFE AND KIDS? THIS IS MY SISTER, SUZY. BOB, SUZY ... SUZY, BOB. OH, YOU'VE MET.

AND THIS IS ... CARLTON, I BELIEVE. CARLTON DOES THIS AMAZING TRICK WITH THE VACUUM CLEANER — YOU HAVE TO SEE IT TO BELIEVE IT. ANYWAY, I'D KNOW THESE GUYS ANYWHERE. DO YOU WANT ME TO ASK THEM IF THEY KNOW YOUR PING-PONG BALL?

REALLY, SAM? I'M DISAPPOINTED.

OH, PLEASE. THAT'S MUM'S LINE.

NO, I'M DISAPPOINTED BECAUSE IF YOU'RE GOING TO BECOME A PROFESSIONAL LIAR, WHICH YOU SEEM DETERMINED TO DO, YOU COULD AT LEAST BE A LITTLE BIT BETTER AT IT.

I AM TELLING THE TRUTH, SIS. IT'S JUST ... THE TRUTH IS COMPLICATED. LIKE AN ELEPHANT.

TOSS!

FLOUNCE →

TACK

TACK

TACK

ROLL...

I suppose it shouldn't be a total surprise that Sis has her doubts. Particularly with what happened a little while after the **IMAGINARY CHEESEBURGER INCIDENT** – which led me straight back into Feeny's bad books for a second time.

The
BREAK
BOX LIE

Since I ruined Feeny's lunchtimes forever, I've managed to stay out of his way – and, honestly, I think the lack of cheeseburgers is doing him some good. Or maybe he's been working out in preparation for my inevitable doom.

But I refrain from comment. In any case, my attention is focused on deepening the frankly not-at-all-deep connection between me and the belle of Parsley Primary, Rhoda Jones.

This makes my schooldays happier all round. Except in one area – the **BREAK BOX**.

This unassuming shoebox of delights is the bane of my life. Every morning, as we troop into class, those who've brought a snack for breaktime plonk it in the Break Box.

These may include:

ED'S WASABI PEAS.
GUARANTEED TO BLOW
YOUR SOCKS OFF.

ABDI'S GOJI BERRIES,
WHICH HIS MUM CALLS
'NATURE'S GUMMYS'.
YEAH, RIGHT...

MARTHA'S PACKET NOODLES.
SHE SPRINKLES THE POWDER
ON THE DRY NOODLES AND
CRUNCHES THEM UP.
IT'S GROSS.

I DON'T KNOW WHAT
THIS IS OR WHO IT
BELONGS TO. IT LIVES
IN THE BREAK BOX.

As you can imagine, coming from a home where non-existent cheeseburgers are better than an actual packed lunch, I'm NEVER in possession of a mid-morning snack.

At breaktime, the break monitor (Rhoda) goes from table to table offering up the Break Box. You're supposed to take whatever is yours. Each day, when Rhoda stops at my table, I make a little flirtatious small talk...

I GOT BITTEN BY A SNAKE YESTERDAY AND THEY HAD TO CUT MY LEG OFF BEFORE THE POISON SPREAD, BUT BECAUSE I HAVE THIS RARE HEALING DISORDER – WELL, IT'S MORE OF A SUPERPOWER REALLY – MY LEG GREW BACK AND...

TWIDDLE!

DID YOU BRING ANYTHING FOR BREAK?

NO.

OKAY, BYE.

PLOP!

Then Rhoda would, reluctantly I think, move on. But I gradually begin to realize that the pangs I feel every day as I watch her retreating figure possibly have as much to do with hunger as love.

LOVE
PECKISHNESS

EXACTLY THE SAME
FEELING, VERY SLIGHTLY
LOWER DOWN...

And one day, when Rhoda waves the Break Box under my nose, I can stand it no longer. I put my hand in, lucky-dip-style, and grab a snack.

RUMMAGE!

Stealing is bad, I know. But I'm *soooo* hungry.

And anyway is it really stealing if you're just taking something completely randomly, without looking?

YEAH, BUDDY, IT'S STEALING.

Well ... anyway.

As luck would have it, I've snaffled a rather exciting prize – a foot-long super-salami meat feast!

NOM NOM NOM

I'm just enjoying the warm afterglow of a processed meat product . . .

. . . when a commotion breaks out further down the room. A loud thumping and a sort of angry griping.

WHERE'S MY FOOT-LONG SUPER-SALAMI MEAT FEAST? IT'S GONE — SOMEONE'S TAKEN IT!

THIS . . . ISN'T . . . HAPPENING.

Meanwhile, Rhoda has called Miss M over to attend the fuss.

Rhoda! Where's your sense of loyalty? I thought we had something!

Well, what would *you* do? I know what I'd do – panic and stick to my guns.

I pick up my trusty **Spade of Lying** and get digging.

So it's my word versus Pete Feeny's... The room goes
very quiet.

The room seems to have got hotter as well as quieter. From deep within, I find some steely resolve (coincidentally, Steely Resolve is the name of Wolfe Stone's motorbike).

Luckily for me, Miss M then throws me a rope ladder. She sends me to go and get Sis...

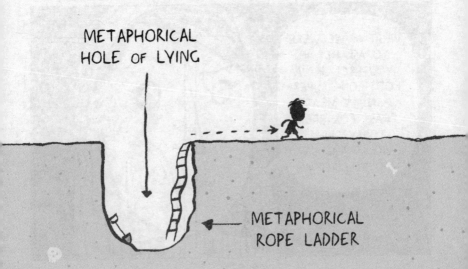

Going to get Sis gives me ample time to plan my next move, and I think of the perfect way to make this work – a bit of Grandpa-style auto-suggestion.

WHAT HAVE YOU DONE NOW, SAM?

WELL. YOU KNOW HOW MUM ALWAYS PACKS ME OFF TO SCHOOL WITH A FOOT-LONG SUPER-SALAMI MEAT FEAST FOR BREAK EVERY DAY?

FIRSTLY – NO.

AND SECONDLY – DEFINITELY NOT.

HMM.

LET'S TAKE THE LONG WAY ROUND.

Sis can charm the birds out of the trees – even Feeny has a soft spot for her. There's just a chance, if she'll back me up, I can avoid certain curtains.

SUZY, DID SAM BRING A FOOT-LONG SUPER-SALAMI MEAT FEAST FOR BREAK TODAY?

SHE LOOKS AT MISS M.

SHE LOOKS AT FEENY.

SHE DOESN'T LOOK AT ME.

She wrestles with her conscience (I've heard that's a thing). Eventually, she speaks.

We've now reached what Wolfe Stone calls a 'stalemate'.

It's bad. I lied. I got my sister to lie for me too. But you can see my dilemma – what would you have done?

And, of course, there's one other person who knows the truth.

In case you're wondering, that's the international symbol for ...

STRIKE TWO!

RALPH - MY PRECIOUS CHINA DOG.

HE USUALLY LIVES ON THE MANTELPIECE. BUT HE'S NOT THERE ANY MORE.

AAAH, THAT RALPH. I'VE NO IDEA.

REALLY? IS THAT TRUE, SAM?

BECAUSE I FOUND THIS EAR UNDER THE SOFA.

EEP! THAT ...THERE?

Sometimes, it's necessary to employ an *advanced distraction technique*. This one I like to call '**LOOK, A SQUIRREL!**'

ALL I CAN SAY FOR SURE IS THAT IT WASN'T ME. CHARLIE AND I WILL PUT OUT AN APB* FOR A DOG WITH A MISSING EAR TOMORROW. WE WILL SOLVE THE MYSTERY – I PROMISE!

*APB. WE HAVE NO IDEA WHAT THIS IS, BUT IT'S SOMETHING THAT HAPPENS IN WOLFE STONE QUITE A LOT.

ANGRY PINK BABOON?

ACCIDENTALLY POISONOUS BREAKFAST?

WHOOPS!

AWFULLY PRETTY BIRTHMARK?

I THINK IT'S BEDTIME FOR YOU, YOUNG MAN.

AND SPEAKING OF PROMISES — YOU CAN TAKE YOUR CAT WITH YOU TOO, WHILE YOU HAVE A GOOD THINK ABOUT THINGS.

I suppose I should explain how Pudding came to be in our lives. And yes, the truth may have been skirted in the process.

The
LIE ABOUT
PUDDING

Now you'll have noticed my mum called Pudding 'YOUR cat'. Well, strictly speaking, she belongs to the entire family. And, honestly, they ought to be grateful to have her.

I know she has problems:

the peeing in the fruit bowl,

the wig-outs,

the binge eating.

But, if you'd seen what she's seen, you might have a few nervous habits yourself...

It's just before Christmas, and shortly after the **Incident of the Foot-Long Super-Salami Meat Feast**. Charlie and I are spending a morning in the park playing *Wolfe Stone and the Incident of the Foot-Long Super-Salami Meat Feast*.

Wolfe (me) has just tracked the salami to a downtown lock-up (old storm drain), only to discover that the thief is none other than his long-time nemesis, Bad Timing Billy (Charlie).

COME ON OUT, BILLY. AND BRING THAT OVERSIZED RECOVERED MEAT SNACK WITH YOU. UNHARMED.

MIOAW

HEY ... IT'S A LITTLE CAT!

WHOA! WITH ... REALLY QUITE ENORMOUS EYES. HEY, LITTLE FELLA. CHARLIE, TAKE ME CLOSER.

OR ... YOU COULD GET DOWN?

RIGHT.

Okay, this is bad. I'm two strikes down, minding my own business as best I can, and all roads seem to lead to Feeny.

THERE'S NO WAY I'M LETTING FEENY'S EVIL DOG GET HIS PAWS ON THAT CAT, CHARLIE. DON'T THOSE EYES REMIND YOU OF SOMEONE? IT'S CARL CURTAINS. THIS CAT IS A VICTIM OF THREE STRIKES FEENY.

BUT YOU'RE TWO STRIKES DOWN YOURSELF — IF FEENY FINDS OUT YOU'VE TAKEN THE CAT, IT'S CURTAINS FOR YOU!

SO I JUST HAVE TO MAKE SURE HE DOESN'T FIND OUT.

But what to do? My parents are unlikely (understatement) to allow me to keep a cat. I can picture the conversation...

However, of course, it's Christmas – and Christmas is the time for giving. And also the time for ingenious gifts.

Time to open presents. I have a combined present for the entire family.

Needless to say, they're speechless with joy.

YES, WONDERFUL ISN'T IT? IT'S A GUATEMALAN INTERNET RESCUE CAT.

THESE CATS LIVE IN THE MOST AWFUL CONDITIONS, FORCED TO PLAY THE PIANO ...

AND REACT BADLY TO CUCUMBERS, ALL FOR THE PLEASURE OF INTERNET VIEWERS.

BY ADOPTING THE CAT, YOU ENSURE THAT IT CAN LIVE OUT THE REST OF ITS LIFE IN PEACE, WITHOUT EVER ONCE HAVING TO WEAR A HALF-MELON ON ITS HEAD FOR THE AMUSEMENT OF STRANGERS.

SAAAM...

THAT MIGHT GET CONFUSING.

EYE... VOR?

IT'S A GIRL.

EYE... LEEN!

MARTIN!

IT'S A GIRL. BESIDES MARTIN IS DAD'S NAME. AGAIN, CONFUSING. GRANDPA?

WHY DO YOU WANT TO CALL IT GRANDPA?

No one in my family likes Christmas pudding, so we have trifle instead.

My dad always makes the same jokes every year.

To try and stop this, my mum calls it pudding, not trifle.

Just as Mum's bringing the trifle/pudding to the table, something bad happens.

At the utterance of the word 'butcher', the Guatemalan big-eyed, no-name internet cat takes a turn for the worse.

She hops out of the box into the fruit bowl, and does a very long wee...

From there, she hops across to the side table and binge-eats an entire bowl of Celebrations, with the wrappers still on.

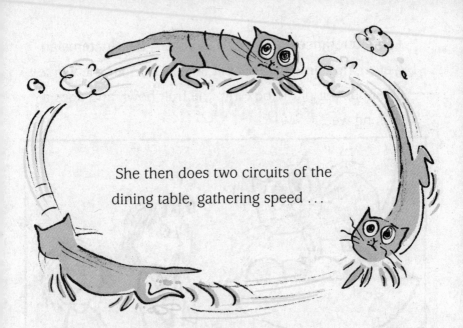

She then does two circuits of the
dining table, gathering speed . . .

. . . before leaping up the wall and back into the middle
of the table . . .

… landing slap-bang in the middle of the ~~trifle!~~, sorry I mean …

… PUDDING!!!!

I try and defuse the situation…

PUDDING!

I LIKE THAT NAME ACTUALLY.

LATER ON CHRISTMAS DAY...

I can guarantee my mum won't believe that Pudding faces certain death at the hands of Feeny and his evil mutt... I have to think fast. And then – inspiration!

So that's how I came to be Pudding's guardian and landed in the jam I'm in now. I'm the only person standing between her and certain demise at the hands of (don't even say the name) – and all I have to do is not lie. But if I tell the truth...

Occasionally, in times of great stress, my inner three-year-old comes out.

HEY, HOW COME YOU WEREN'T AT SCHOOL YESTERDAY?

EYE TEST, REMEMBER?

OH YEAH, HOW DID THAT GO?

I...I THINK I SEE ONE!

APPARENTLY, MY EYES ARE IN THERE SOMEWHERE. WHICH IS A HUGE RELIEF FOR MY MUM — YOU KNOW HOW SHE WORRIES. I KNEW THEY WERE THERE. I MEAN, I CAN SEE STUFF.

...I GOT THIS HANDY TELESCOPE. IT'S AMAZING – EVERYTHING'S SOOO CLEAR!

WHOA! THOSE NOSE HAIRS COULD USE A TRIM. DID I MISS MUCH AT SCHOOL?

YESTERDAY AT SCHOOL WAS WHAT MY MUM WOULD CALL ...

'EVENTFUL'.

OR AS WOLFE STONE WOULD PUT IT:

'EVENTFUL'.

BOOM!

WE HAD SHOW-AND-TELL, REMEMBER? I TOOK THE PLASTIC FORK I USED TO SINGLE-HANDEDLY DEFEAT POSEIDON, LORD OF THE DEEP?

RINGS A BELL...

WELL, ANYWAY, I DIDN'T GET TO GO.

OKAY, PETER, YOU'RE NEXT FOR SHOW-AND-TELL. SAM, YOU CAN GO AFTERWARDS.

TODAY I WILL DEMONSTRATE BUTCHER'S AMAZING CAT-SEEKING ABILITIES.

IT'S CLEAR WHAT'S GOING ON HERE. FEENY WANTS TO CONFIRM HIS SUSPICIONS THAT I TOOK THE CAT.

HE WAS LOOKING RIGHT AT ME.

BUT I WAS LOOKING RIGHT BACK AT HIM.

THANK YOU, PETER — THAT'S VERY IMPRESSIVE. NOW IT'S SAM'S TURN.

OH YEAH, SAM LYTTLE, LYTTLE LIAR...

SAM'S TURN IT IS, ALL RIGHT.

SO HE COMES TOWARDS ME WITH BUTCHER... AND I'M SECONDS AWAY FROM DISCOVERY. AND THERE'S NOTHING I CAN DO TO STOP IT.

I GET SLOWLY TO MY FEET...

GRRRRRR...

123

WOW. THIS IS A BIT LIKE THE EPISODE OF WOLFE STONE WHERE HE TRIES TO SMUGGLE THE MICROFILM OUT OF BAD TIMING BILLY'S HEADQUARTERS.

OH. YEAH. I GUESS IT IS A BIT LIKE THAT. IT HADN'T OCCURRED TO ME.

SAY THAT AGAIN. . .

FEENY'S HAND GRIPS THE CHAIR BEHIND HIM.

I FIX HIM WITH A GIMLET-EYED STARE AND REPEAT WHAT I SAID.

WOW — DIDN'T HE TURN THE DEAD EYE ON YOU?

YEAH, BUT IT DIDN'T BOTHER ME FOR A MINUTE.

THE EXACT SAME WAY WOLFE STONE DEFEATED COPPERHEAD CODY IN 'SNAKEBITE'.

OH YEAH, I SEE THE SIMILARITY. ANYWAY ... FEENY STAGGERS ROUND THE CLASSROOM, WITH BUTCHER TANGLED ROUND HIS LEGS. AND I CASUALLY OPEN THE CLASSROOM DOOR BEHIND ME AND SAY ...

BUTCHER, LOOK – A SQUIRREL!

GRRR... WOOF! WOOF!

BUTCHER ZOOMS OUT THE DOOR, DRAGGING FEENY BEHIND HIM, OUT OF THE SCHOOL GATES. EVERYONE CHEERS!

SOUNDS LIKE A TRIUMPH FOR TRUTH AND JUSTICE! FOR YEARS TO COME, THE KIDS WILL BE TALKING ABOUT THE TIME SAM LYTTLE SHOWED AND TOLD PETER FEENY, THE PERIL OF PARSLEY PRIMARY!

HEH HEH. YEAH...

Is a lie still a lie, even if you don't tell it?

What I mean is – if someone believes something, and you know it's not strictly true but you don't tell them, is that lying? Let me give you an example, but be prepared – this one's pretty gross...

The
POISON
GAS
CLOUD
LIE

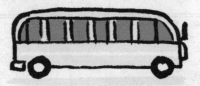

Every year in the Christmas hols, Mum puts Sis and me on a coach to go and stay with our cousins, Bill and Becky, for a few days.

~~BECKY~~ BILL   ~~BILL~~ BECKY

This particular year, the journey makes me feel really sick. At least I have Sis to take care of me...

By the time we arrive at Bill and Becky's, it's clear it isn't just travel sickness.

My Aunt Ruthie puts me straight to bed in a cosy room.

And there I stay, getting greener by the hour, for the next two days.

The thing is, I'm not actually sick but I can't eat, and I can't go to the toilet. I'm like a putrid puffball waiting to pop.

Sis and the cousins do their best to keep my spirits up.

At least my lovely Aunt Ruthie is there for me.

Finally, on the third day, my fever breaks and I begin to feel better. My loved ones gather at my bedside.

Suddenly, from deep within my pyjamas comes a low rumbling ...

... that turns into a sort of gurgling ...

... and then a quieter version of the noise a walrus makes when it's having a baby walrus ... followed by an eerie silence.

And then ...

It's hard to tell if the others are laughing or crying, gagging or just suffering the effects of a newly invented nerve gas – one that makes you laugh and cry and gag all at the same time.

But, as the air eventually clears, I can see they are, despite the revulsion, sort of impressed by the power of my silent-but-deadly gas cloud.

For years afterwards, whenever we see Bill and Becky, we all talk about the incredible lasting effects of the worst stench ever created by a human being.

REMEMBER THAT FART YOU DID WHEN YOU WERE ILL AT OUR HOUSE? AFTER YOU LEFT, THE WALLPAPER STARTED TO PEEL AND THE TV STOPPED WORKING. MUM HAD TO HAVE THE CARPET REPLACED. IT WAS AWESOME!!!

YEAH, HEH HEH. IT WAS PRETTY SPECIAL. WHAT CAN I SAY?

I'm happy to bask in the glory and never let them know the actual truth, because it is so horrifying that I've never told anyone. Until now.

So, if you don't think you can handle it, just shut the book and walk away – no hard feelings.

Otherwise, bring your ear close to the page and I'll whisper it. The truth is. . .

It was the mother of all *silent-but-deadly*, **rotten-egg**-with-**rancid-radishes**-and-a-side-order-of-**burnt-armpit-hair** burps. To produce such a monstrosity from your bum? Well, that makes you a legend. But from your mouth?

The mouth that may have kissed you on the cheek? May have shared the straw in your milkshake?

It's just wrong.

Best swept under the carpet.

And have the carpet replaced.

You probably won't have noticed this, but my mum is giving off subtle hints that she thinks I'm somehow involved with the missing potatoes.

It's time to speak up.

1) A PIECE OF SPORTING EQUIPMENT APPEAR IN THE JAR OF PEANUT BUTTER.

2) RALPH, MUM'S BELOVED CHINA DOG, STRANGELY REDUCED IN STATURE TO THE SIZE OF A SINGLE EAR.

3) AN ENTIRE BAG OF POTATOES OF THE KING EDWARD VARIETY, HAND-GROWN WITH PASSION AND FORBEARANCE BY OUR OWN BELOVED GRANDPA, MYSTERIOUSLY TAKEN A TURN FOR THE GONE.

THREE SEEMINGLY UNRELATED OCCURRENCES — OR ARE THEY?

OF COURSE THEY AREN'T.

I CAN NOW, TO EVERYONE'S SATISFACTION, REVEAL THE TRUTH BEHIND THESE MYSTERIES ONCE AND FOR ALL.

GOSH, WELL DONE, SAM.

ABOUT TIME TOO.

IT GIVES ME NO GREAT PLEASURE TO TELL YOU THIS — FRANKLY, I'M EMBARRASSED IT'S TAKEN ME SO LONG TO COME TO THIS POINT...

GET IT OFF YOUR CHEST, SAMMY!

GOOD FOR YOU, SAM!

YES, WE'RE ALL THINKING THE SAME THING. WE ALL KNOW WHO'S BEHIND THESE MYSTERIOUS MISDEMEANOURS...

SAM.

SAM.

SAM.

SAM.

SAM.

THAT'S RIGHT...

CLICK!

A POLTERGEIST!

I'M AFRAID THERE'S NO OTHER PLAUSIBLE EXPLANATION. THINK ABOUT IT: NO MERE MORTAL — NOT EVEN GRANDPA — COULD MAKE SEVERAL KILOS OF SPUDS DISAPPEAR INTO THIN AIR. AND THERE'S PLENTY OF EVIDENCE TO SUGGEST THAT, WHEN POLTERGEISTS MOVE VERY FAST, THEY CREATE ECTOPLASMIC AIR CURRENTS THAT COULD PLAUSIBLY KNOCK A CHINA DOG CLEAN INTO AN ALTERNATE DIMENSION. NOW I KNOW WHAT YOU'RE THINKING...

SAM DID IT.

COME ON, SAM, DO THE DECENT THING.

SAMMY, 'FESS UP. YOU'LL FEEL BETTER FOR IT.

THIS IS PITIFUL.

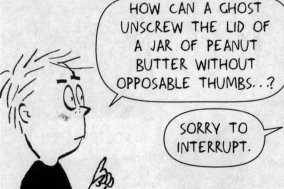

HOW CAN A GHOST UNSCREW THE LID OF A JAR OF PEANUT BUTTER WITHOUT OPPOSABLE THUMBS...?

SORRY TO INTERRUPT.

148

SHALL WE HIT THE PARK?

HEY, HOW ABOUT WE DON'T GO THERE? I DO NOT WANT TO RISK RUNNING INTO FEENY.

BUT, AFTER THE WOLFE STONE-STYLE SCHOOLING YOU GAVE HIM ON FRIDAY, HE'LL NEVER TERRORIZE ANYONE EVER AGAIN!

OH – RIIIGHT. BUT IT'S – YOU KNOW – I FEEL BAD FOR THE GUY REALLY. HE PROBABLY NEEDS SOME THINKING TIME.

OKAY, LET'S GO TO THE OLD PARK INSTEAD. NO ONE EVER GOES THERE.

The 'old' park *was* the park until they built the
new park. We all used to love it when it was all we had.

The steps up the slide
had no handrail.

The swings were too close to
the roundabout, so you had
to time your
swinging
to miss the
spinning kids...

The **new park** changed all that. Proper handrails; bouncy rubber floor; swings with harnesses – a good park ruined.

They're supposed to be tearing the **OLD PARK** down, but it hasn't happened yet – the roundabout has seized up and the slide has fallen on its side, but it still has a certain charm.

Butcher went nuts when he got to me, confirming Feeny's suspicions.

So, after school, I didn't hang around – I hightailed it home as soon as the bell went. I kept checking behind me and Feeny wasn't following.

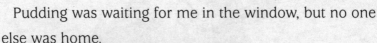

Pudding was waiting for me in the window, but no one else was home.

IT'S OKAY, PUDDING, HE DOESN'T KNOW WHERE WE LIVE.

Butcher must have picked up my scent. I was caught red-handed!

FEENY MADE THE INTERNATIONAL SIGN FOR STRIKE THREE.

THEN HE MADE THE INTERNATIONAL SIGN FOR CURTAINS.

Then ... he put the dead eye on me. I had to look away.

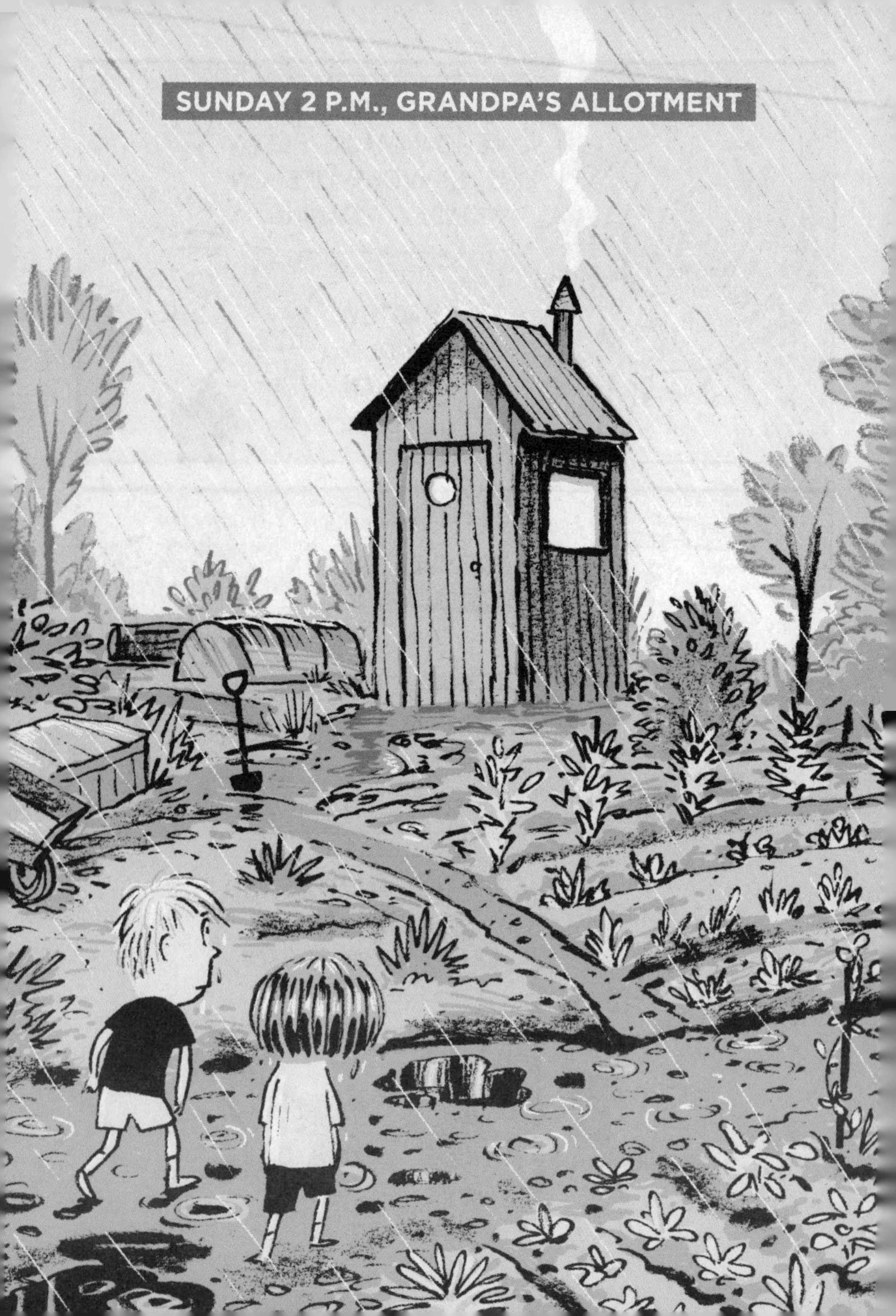
SUNDAY 2 P.M., GRANDPA'S ALLOTMENT

THIS FEENY PROBLEM — IT ALL STARTED WITH THE IMAGINARY CHEESEBURGER, DIDN'T IT?

YES.

HMMM...

WELL...

IN THAT CASE...

I DON'T KNOW.

HMMM.

HO!

BUT YOU'VE GOT TO MAKE ME A PROMISE...

NOTHING TO DO WITH RADISHES, I HOPE.

ONCE THIS BUSINESS IS DONE WITH ON MONDAY, YOU NEED TO TELL THE TRUTH ABOUT THE SHENANIGANS AT HOME. THE PING-PONG BALL, THE CHINA DOG — AND ESPECIALLY MY SPUDS. THE TRUTH, THE WHOLE TRUTH AND NOTHING BUT THE TRUTH.

BUT GRANDPA... IT'S JUST, WELL, THE TRUTH IS ... COMPLICATED.

I KNOW, I KNOW — LIKE AN ELEPHANT.

EXACTLY!

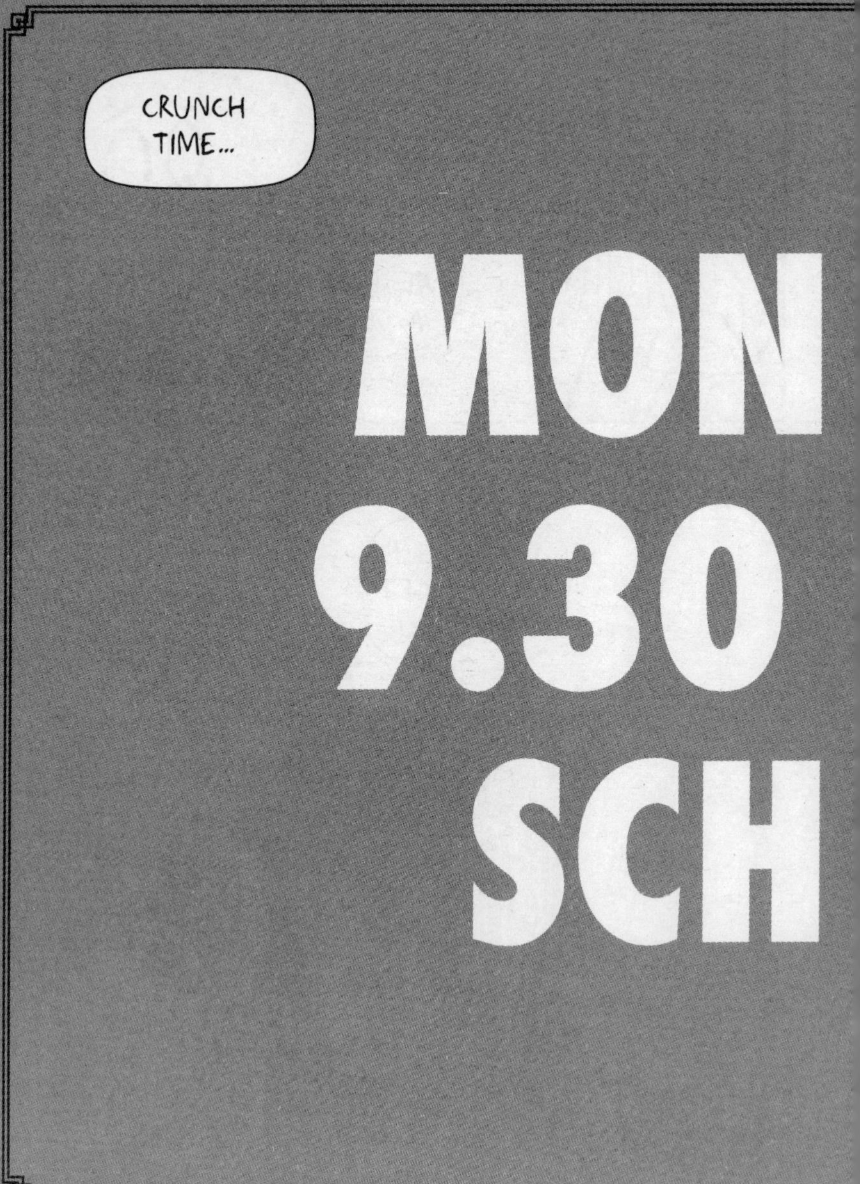
CRUNCH TIME...
MON
9.30
SCH

DAY A.M. OOL

GULP!

OKAY, CLASS. SAM, WHO DIDN'T GET TO SHOW-AND-TELL ON FRIDAY, IS GOING TO DO A VERY UNUSUAL ONE FOR US THIS MORNING.

TODAY I WILL DEMONSTRATE THE AMAZING POWER OF HYPNOSIS - AS PERFECTED BY MY GRANDFATHER, THE GREAT WONDEROSO...

I NEED A VOLUNTEER FROM THE AUDIENCE.

ANYONE ELSE?

THIS IS RUBBISH! EVERYONE KNOWS CHARLIE AND SAM ARE FRIENDS. CHARLIE'S A STOOGE!

UM...

MUNCH MUNCH!

IT'S JUST ANOTHER STUPID LIE!

IT'S NOT, IT'S REAL...

COME ON, TAKE THE BAIT...

WELL, IF IT'S SO REAL, IT'LL WORK ON ME, WON'T IT?

PHEW! THAT'S THE PLAN.

YES, I THINK WE CAN PROBABLY HAVE ONE MORE DEMONSTRATION. TO REFUTE THE CHARGES OF MR FEENY.

YOU MIGHT AS WELL GET SHOWN UP AS THE LYTTLE LIAR YOU ARE — BEFORE CURTAINS TIME.

GULP!

THAT ISN'T AN APPLE AT ALL. EVERYONE HERE CAN SEE IT'S NOT. WHY DON'T YOU TAKE A BITE? THEN YOU'LL REALIZE WHAT I MEAN.

FINE, I'LL TAKE A BITE OF THE APPLE!

YOU SEE, IT'S NOT AN APPLE AT ALL, IS IT?

CRUNCH!

SIT DOWN NOW BOYS.

ACTUALLY, CAN I KEEP THE, ER ... APPLE, MISS?

OKAY, CLASS, MATHS TEXTBOOKS, PLEASE!

SNARFLE!

MISS, CAN I GO TO THE LOO, PLEASE?

YES, CHARLIE, BUT HURRY UP NOW.

SNARF! SNAFFLE!

SKWEE   SKWEE   *SKWEE...*

SKWEE   SKWEE   *SKWEE...*

RUMMAGE!
RUMMAGE!

WHEN FEENY IMAGINES A CHEESEBURGER
AT THE SAME TIME AS EATING ONE,
HE WILL HAVE THE INSTANT QUEASIES.
ONCE YOU'VE SHOWN HIM THE POWER
YOU HOLD, HE'LL WANT TO GIVE YOU
AS WIDE A BERTH AS POSSIBLE.
HE'LL NEVER BOTHER YOU,
OR YOUR CAT, AGAIN.

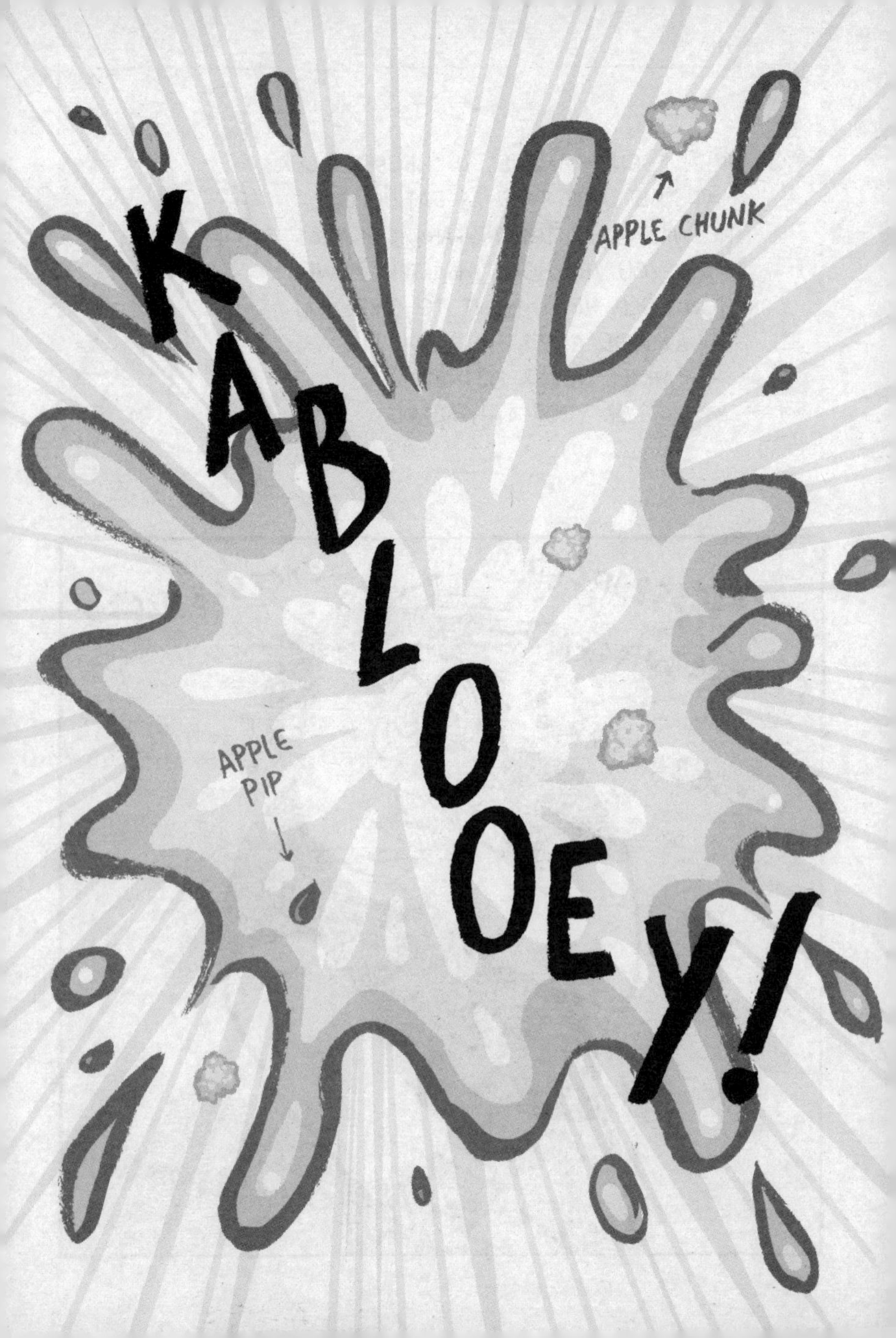
KABLOOEY!
APPLE CHUNK
APPLE PIP

PLUS, HE KNOWS I HAVE THE POWER OF THE CHEESEBURGER AT MY FINGERTIPS. WE'RE ALL SAFE, FOR THE MOMENT. THANKS FOR ALL YOUR HELP, CHARLIE — CAN I BUY YOU A LOLLY?

I'M STUFFED. I'VE BEEN EATING CHOCOLATE BARS ALL AFTERNOON. I CAN'T GET ENOUGH OF THEM.

OOPS!

BESIDES, YOU NEED TO GET HOME — YOU HAVE YOUR SIDE OF THE BARGAIN TO KEEP, REMEMBER?

RIGHT. HOW COULD I FORGET?

TOOT!
TOOT!

AHEM. ANYWAY, I OBVIOUSLY HAD A LOT OF STEAM TO WORK OFF. THE SHOTS JUST KEPT GETTING MORE AND MORE POWERFUL, AND I HAD TO RUN FURTHER AND FURTHER TO BAT THEM BACK. BUT, TRY AS I MIGHT, I COULDN'T WEAR MY OPPONENT DOWN. NEITHER OF US COULD.

I FINALLY SAW MY CHANCE TO DELIVER AN UNRETURNABLE SMASH.

KER-
SMASH!

EXCEPT I'D FORGOTTEN HOW GOOD I AM AT THIS GAME. THE BALL BOUNCED ON THE SIDE TABLE IN THE LIVING ROOM (THAT'S ALLOWED) AND, BEFORE I KNEW IT, THERE I WAS — READY TO MAKE THE RETURN.

BUT I MUST HAVE MISJUDGED MY BACKHAND. I SWIPED RALPH AND IT WAS GAME OVER.

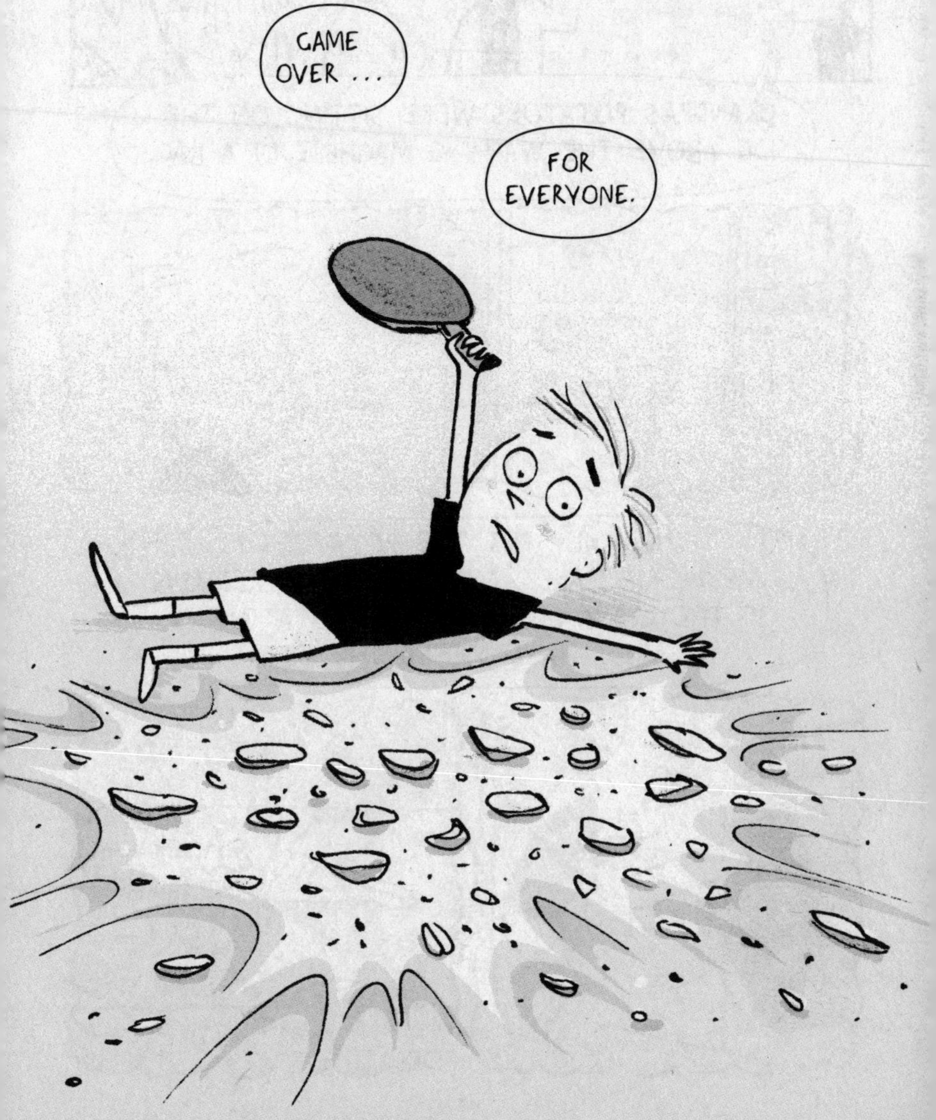
GAME OVER ...
FOR EVERYONE.

OH, SAM!

GRANDPA'S POTATOES WERE SITTING ON THE SIDE ABOVE THE WASHING MACHINE IN A BAG.

I QUICKLY PUT THE POTATOES SOMEWHERE 'SAFE', AND SWEPT THE REMAINS OF THE CHINA DOG INTO THE POTATO BAG. I MUST HAVE MISSED THE EAR.

OH, SAM... WHY DIDN'T YOU SAY SOMETHING AT THE TIME?

SHALL I PLAY SOMETHING POIGNANT YET HOPEFUL ON MY GUITAR?

NO, MARTIN!

I DIDN'T WANT TO GET INTO TROUBLE.

YOU CAN EAT THE MASH AS A PUNISHMENT — I'M CERTAINLY NOT GOING TO. BUT WHAT ABOUT THE PING-PONG BALL IN THE PEANUT BUTTER?

WELL, THAT MUST BE WHERE IT LANDED AFTER THE UNRETURNABLE RETURNED SMASH. BUT WHO, I ASK YOU, LEFT THE LID OFF THE PEANUT BUTTER IN THE FIRST PLACE?

PROBABLY YOU?

FAIR POINT.

HOW DO YOU FEEL, SAMMY BOY?

I FEEL ... I ACTUALLY FEEL ... OKAY.

I MEAN, I FEEL SORRY FOR ALL THE TROUBLE I'VE CAUSED, AND ASHAMED THAT IT TOOK ME SO LONG TO TELL THE TRUTH. BUT I FEEL LIKE ... I FEEL AS THOUGH A WEIGHT HAS DISAPPEARED FROM MY SHOULDERS. FOR THE SECOND TIME TODAY.

THING IS, SAM, WE ALWAYS THINK IT'S YOU ANYWAY, SO YOU'RE REALLY ONLY LYING TO YOURSELF.

I'M PROUD OF YOU, SAM. WE ALL ARE.

At this point, I decide
to leave the proceedings.

My work is done.

And, <u>to be honest</u>,
I do feel as though a
weight has been lifted.

WHICH YOU'RE NOT...

I can see the point of all this 'honesty'.
There's a time and a place for it.

But, if you want
<u>to know the truth</u>, I think
there's a time and
a place for lying too.

DON'T ASK SAM!

Like I said at the start, the truth is complicated. Like an elephant.

In this case, like an elephant with really, really huge eyes.

And whiskers. And some self-control issues.

MEOW...

TRUTH

The
TRUTH
ABOUT
PUDDING

All I'm saying is it might not have gone down *exactly* as I said it to my family.

Pudding *might* have been involved.

Pudding *might* have wigged out when she heard Butcher outside the window and done a giant pee in the bag of potatoes.

She *might* have then binge-eaten the jar of peanut butter and got her head stuck . . .

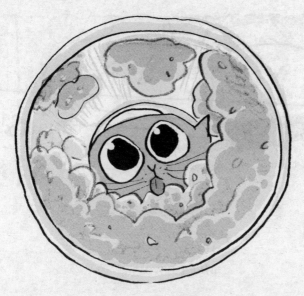

. . . panicked and run circuits of the living room, faster and faster, picking up speed, with me chasing her to get the jar off her face . . .

... finally reaching maximum velocity and knocking Ralph off the mantelpiece.

I'm just saying.

Might have.

Then I *might* have stuck the potatoes in the washing machine and used the cat-pee potato bag to clear up the bits of dog and put the whole lot in the bin outside.

I *might* have missed an ear.

I *might* have stuck a grubby ping-pong ball in the peanut butter to ward off snackers – you've seen where else cats put their tongues, right? I'm thoughtful that way.

So, if that *did* happen, you'd understand my dilemma. If I told the whole truth, Pudding would have to go. But, if my family knew I'd lied, well, that would break my promise and Pudding would have to go.

But for now, at least, Pudding can stay. And that's good for me – those eyes really do help keep me on the straight and narrow.

You can't lie to a cat, it seems.

And me? I just hope I can deal with those elephants as and when they appear. Besides, I like telling stories – people *LIKE* stories.

But sometimes, I suppose, people like to hear the truth.

The End
(for now.)

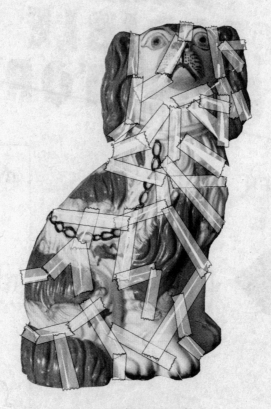

IN MEMORY OF

Ralph

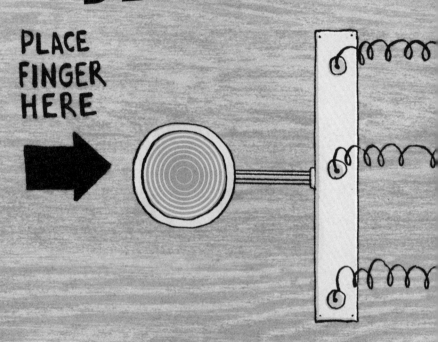

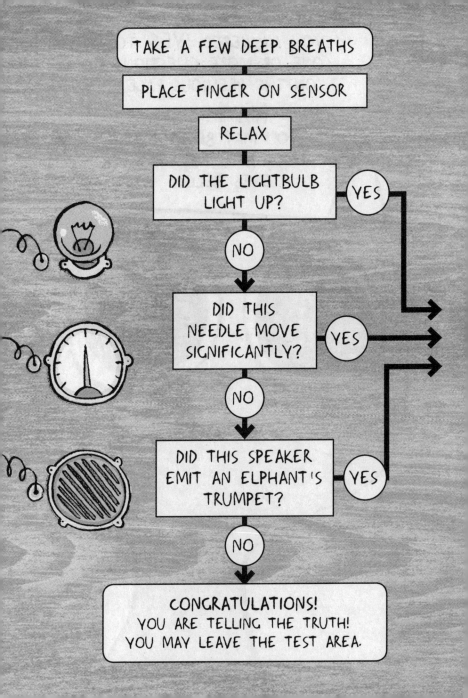

NOW REPEAT
THE TEST...

MEET THE AUTHOR

JOE BERGER

Photograph © Henning Löhlein

I'd like to be able to tell you that this story is entirely made up, and that Sam bears no resemblance to the young me; I'd like to tell you that I didn't, as a boy, share Sam's love of lying. But that would be, well ... a lie. What *is* true is that ever since I was a boy I've wanted to create cartoon stories, and now I'm lucky enough to draw cartoons for a job. Hooray!